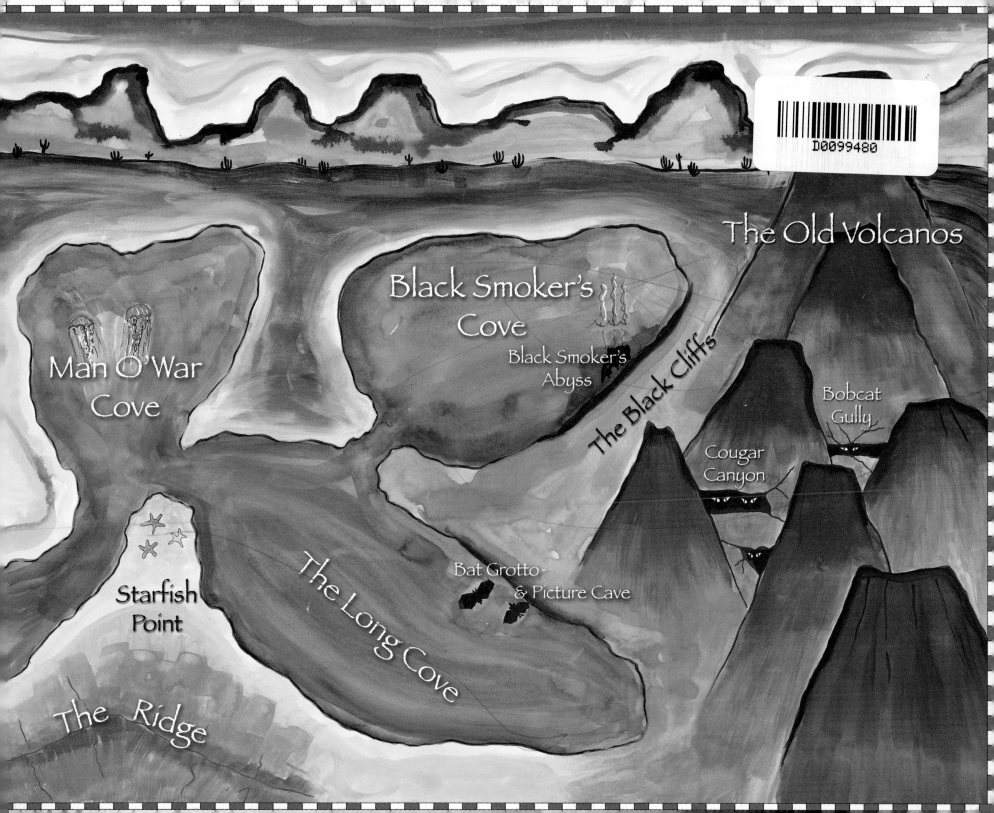

The Old Volcanos

Black Smoker's
Cove

Black Smoker's
Abyss

The Black Cliffs

Man O'War
Cove

Bobcat
Gully

Cougar
Canyon

Bat Grotto
& Picture Cave

Starfish
Point

The Long Cove

The Ridge

Zonk and the Secret Lagoon

The further adventures of Zonk the Dreaming Tortoise.

by David Hoobler

Zonk and the Secret Lagoon,

the further adventures of Zonk the Dreaming Tortoise

by David Hoobler

Many thanks to Gillette Edmunds, Marian Lindner, Rennie Kirby, and Stan Tusan.

This is book two in the Zonk picture book series.

Zonk Galleries and Publishing
3760 Park Boulevard Way Suite 31
Oakland, CA 94610

www.zonktheturtle.com

First edition, second printing 2009
ISBN10: 0-9706537-1-9
ISBN13: 978-0-9706537-1-0

Summary: Zonk finds the ocean. He makes new friends and has new adventures.

The Gulf of California

Zonk's new adventure takes place in the Gulf of California, also know as the Sea of Cortez. A gulf is a part of the ocean extending inland. Much of the Sea of Cortez is surrounded by desert.

For Jorge Luis
+ Nicolas,
An ocean
adventure,
enjoy!,

[signature]

5/5/13

Mexico

The Gulf of California

Baja Peninsula

Pacific Ocean

"You're it!" Zonk shouted. Zonk, Fish and Vaquita were playing tag, racing through the water.

Zonk's dream had come true, he'd found the ocean. He met Fish and many new friends.

They stopped to say "Hi!" to the angelfish, but all he did was blink at them.

"He's a grump," Zonk told Fish. Then Zonk and Fish went off to explore and play some more.

"Watch this," said Zonk then he somersaulted right past the gray whale.

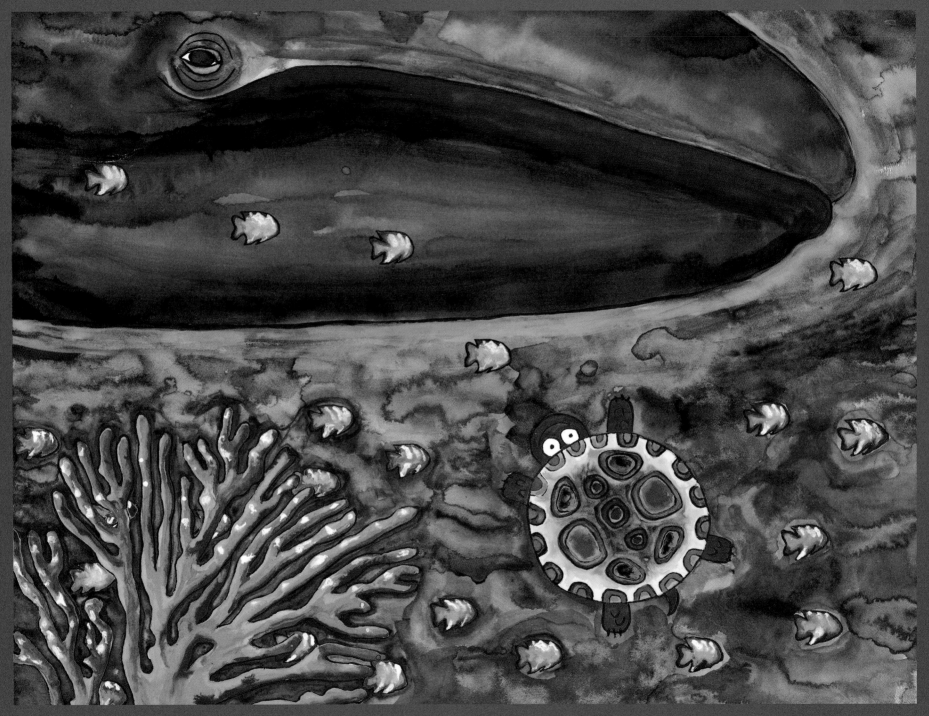

Zonk liked to show off. In the water he felt light as a feather.

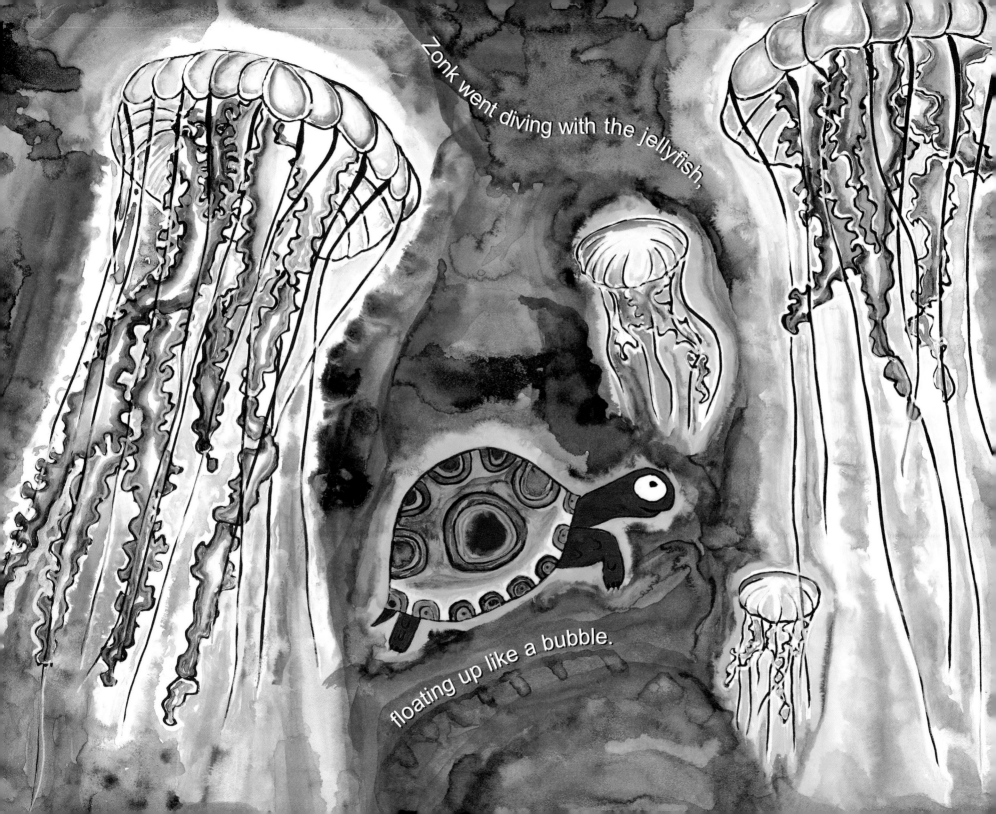

When he got tired, Zonk slept on the beach and dreamt of home.

Zonk missed his family and friends.

One night Zonk felt a bump under his shell.

He woke up frightened.

Zonk was always afraid of monsters under his bed.

The sand in front of Zonk began to move. A nose and a pair of eyes poked through.

A baby sea turtle was crawling out of her nest.

The baby looked up, saw Zonk and said, "Mom."

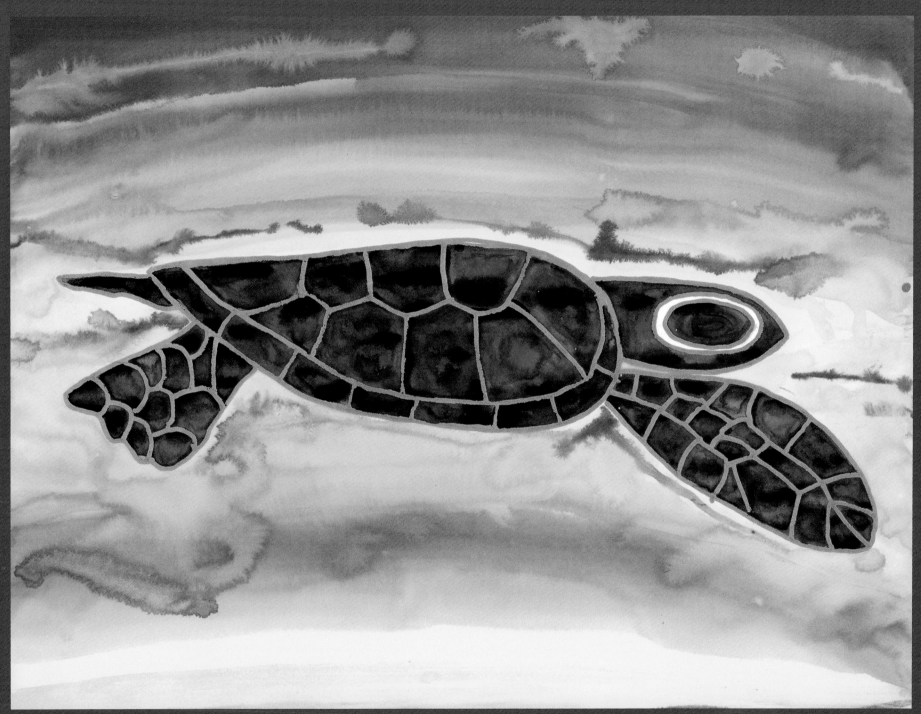

Before Zonk could utter a word the beach exploded with life.

Up and down the beach baby turtles were digging out of nests and heading for the waves. Birds and crabs swooped down gobbling up the little turtles.

A bird clawed Zonk's shell and a crab nipped his nose. "Quick," he shouted. "Into the water."

In the water, away from the crabs and birds, large fish lurked about and this worried Zonk.

"Mom?" said the little turtle.
"No, no, no, I'm not your mom," Zonk replied.
"Come on, follow me. I see a cave."

"Careful, don't step on my fin!" It was Fish. He had been hiding in the cave too.
"Oops. Sorry." said Zonk. "This baby turtle crawled out from under my bed. We need a safe place."
"Hey look, a tunnel. Let's see where it goes," said Zonk.

The tunnel was long and dark with a faint light at the end. Fearsome eyes glared out all around them. "Moray eels," Fish warned in a whisper. "Quick, don't let them catch you." The tunnel became narrower and brighter and they suddenly popped out into a beautiful lagoon.

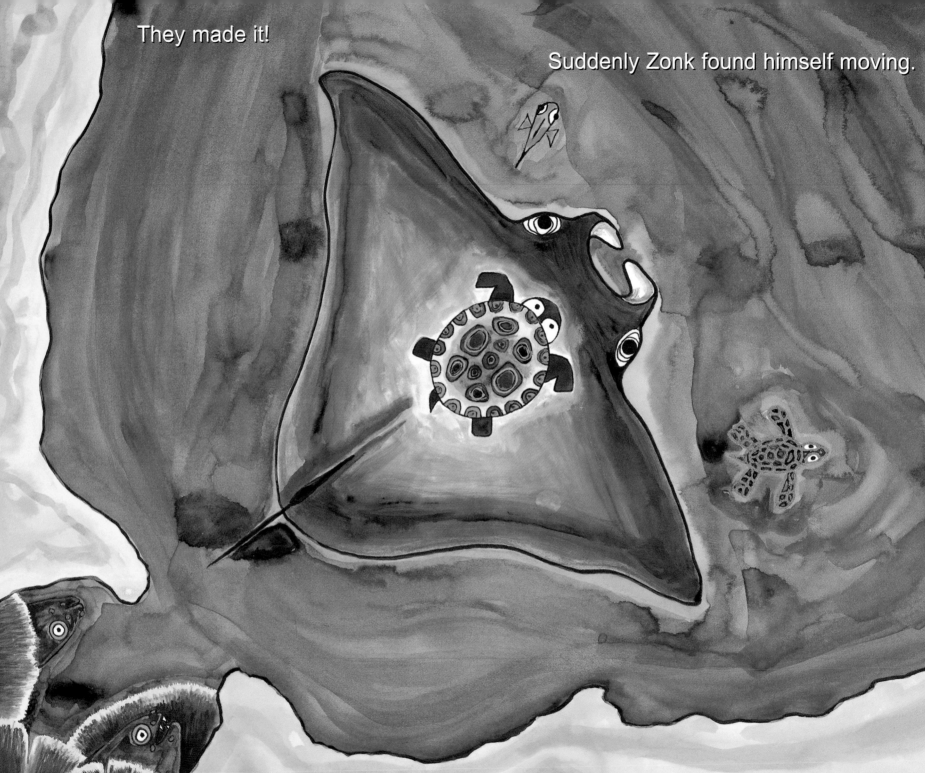

They made it!

Suddenly Zonk found himself moving.

Zonk had stepped onto a manta ray.

"Hang on," said the manta ray. "I'm learning to fly."
Zonk was thrilled as they soared over the waves.

They came to an island covered in crabs, starfish and pelicans. Schools of small fish surrounded the island. As Zonk climbed onto a rock a chorus of questions rained down on them.

"Who are you?"

"Where are you from?"

"How did you get past the moray eels?"

"Are you going to stay?"

"I am Zonk the Sea Tortoise. I come from the desert. These are my friends, Fish and uh..." Zonk realized the baby didn't have a name so he blurted out. "Emily!" "She needs a safe home."

"You may stay," said the Pelican, "but only if you eat sea grass. No eating one another in the Secret Lagoon. And you must look after the baby."

"Thank you for your kindness," replied Zonk, but inside he felt stuck. More and more Zonk was feeling homesick for his family and friends.

The manta ray swam by and asked, "Would you like me to show you around?"

"Sure," said Zonk and he jumped onto the manta ray's back.

All together they began to explore their magical new home. The manta ray continued to practice his flying.

"Everyone calls me Manta," he explained to Zonk. "I am learning to fly so I can leave this lagoon," Manta told Zonk. "I want to go out to the open ocean and meet other manta rays."

Zonk told Manta about the monsoon, the flash flood, and the river that had carried him to the sea. He told him of his dreams, becoming homesick.

"I want to go home and tell everyone about the ocean and my new friends. They won't make fun of me now."

"Can't you just go back up the river you came down?" Manta asked.

"I've traveled so far, I don't know where the river is anymore." Zonk replied.

"Let's go ask the long nose bats where it is," said Manta Ray. "They were the ones that told me about the ocean outside the lagoon."

The bats lived in a water filled cave.
They were daytime sleepers and woke up really cranky.
"There are no rivers in the desert. Go away! Let us sleep."

As they left the cave they
discovered a painting on a wall.
Zonk pointed excitedly and shouted,
"It's Bunny, Snake and Coyote with Vaquita!"
As his voice echoed through the cave, Zonk thought
he heard the walls say, "Come home, Zonk, come home."

Zonk was playing with the Men O'War when Manta got an idea. "Let's go ask the Black Smoker."

Zonk and Manta went to the
Cove of the Black Smoker.

They began to dive down.
"Don't breathe the bubbles,"
Manta warned, "they're bad."

Down and down they went,
into the cold, dark, deep ocean,
all the way to the bottom of
the Black Smoker's Abyss.

A black chimney towered up out of the sea floor belching black smoke and boiling the seawater. Giant clams, guard crabs, and tubeworms surrounded the tower.

"What's that?" Zonk asked, he was really frightened.

"It's The Black Smoker, Spirit of the Lagoon. Go ahead, ask your question," said Manta.

"Where is the river, how can I get home?" Zonk asked.

"We only know what we know," came bubbling out of the smoke.

"We only know what we know; what does that mean?" asked Manta.

"Oh no!" said Zonk. "I don't know what it means, but I've heard it before."

Bewildered and discouraged, Zonk and Manta raced to the surface and back to the island.

When they got to the island the lagoon was in an uproar. Everyone was yelling, "Spit it out. Spit it out." Emily had a baby crab in her mouth.

"She's eating the baby crabs, you have to leave," said the Pelican.

"Oh boy," thought Zonk. "This sea turtle is a lot of trouble. We need to find a family for her."

Zonk and Fish considered going back through the tunnel. "I don't think we could make it past the eels again," said Fish. "Anyway, I'm not going back in there."

Zonk had an idea, "Manta, can you fly us out?"

"I guess this is as good a time as any," said Manta. "Will you climb the ridge and signal the best spot to clear it?"

"Okay," said Zonk and he started up the ridge. Zonk reached the top, finding the best spot to clear the ridge, he signaled to the rest.

Manta began swimming from the far end of the lagoon, racing toward Zonk. When he reached the edge of the water Manta launched himself into the air. Up and up they flew, over the ridge, yelling, "Oh no!!!!"
Just barely missing Zonk's head, they glided down into the waves.

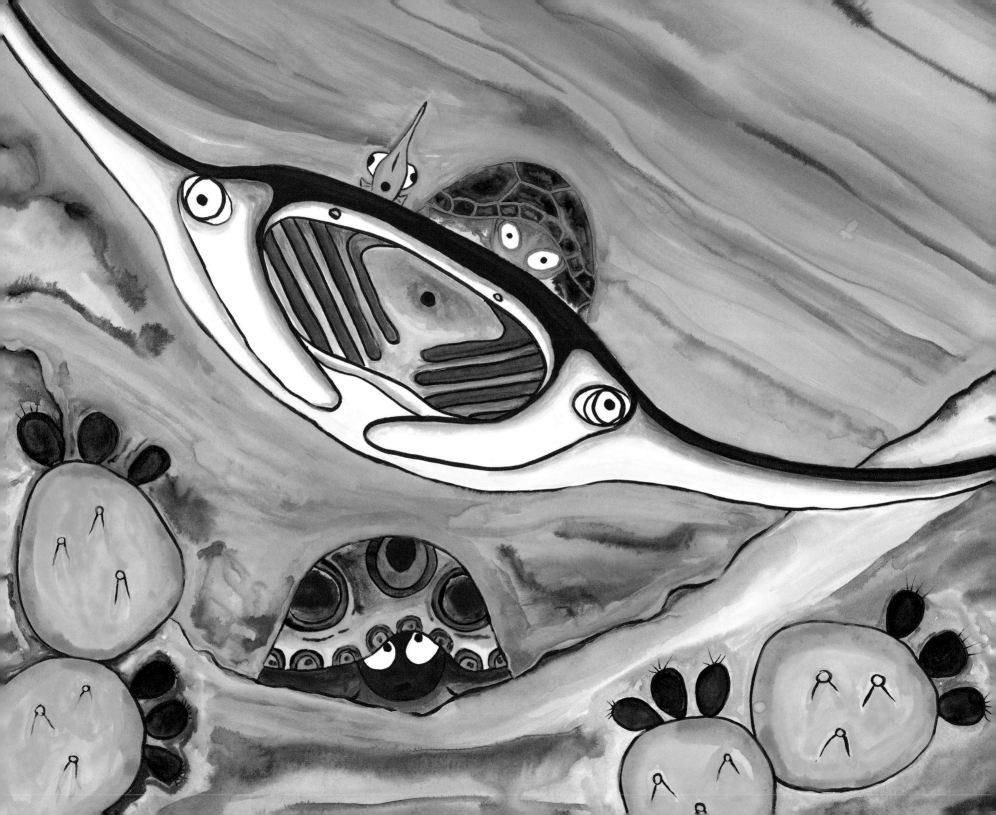

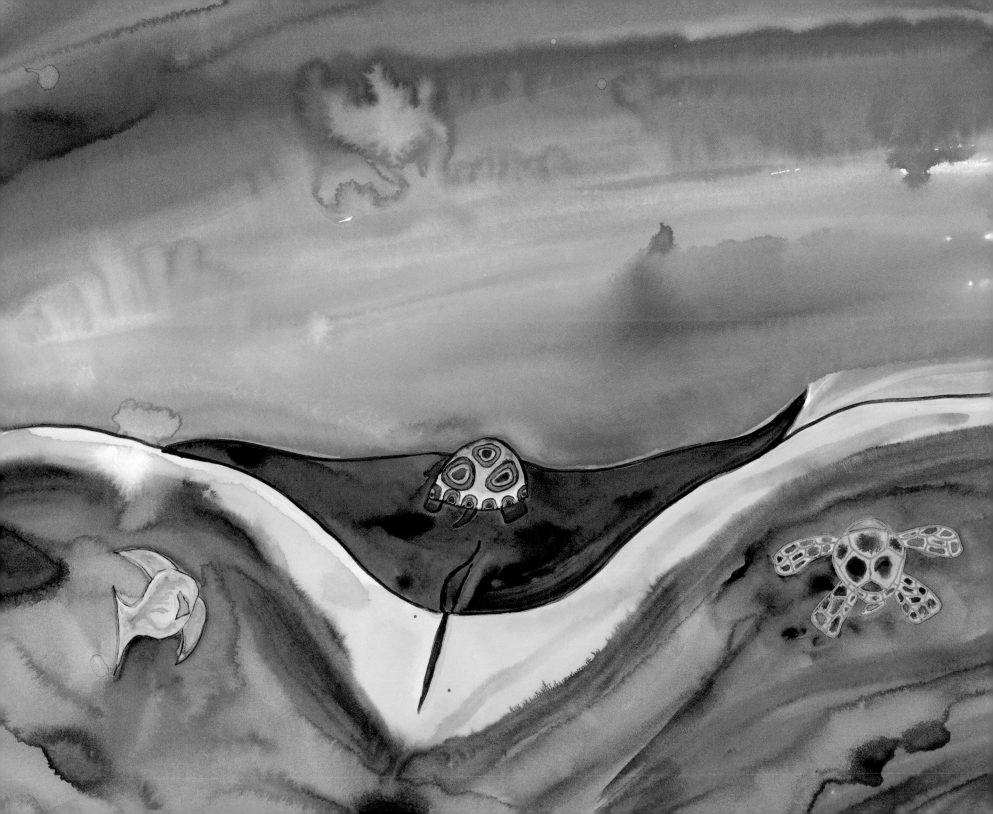

Zonk jumped on Manta's back and the explorers
joined together for their next adventure: to find
the river, the sea turtles and the manta rays.

The Sea of Cortez and Sonoran Desert have been damaged.
They have been damaged by people being careless with nature.
The characters in this book live in the Sea of Cortez
and the Sonoran Desert and they need our help.
We need to always be careful with nature or
the Gray Whale, Emily, Vaquita and the
Long Nose Bats might disappear.

The Gray Whale is doing really well. That is because mankind decided to take care of the Gray Whale, who was terribly endangered at one time. The Gray Whale is a great lesson in how people can help save our environment, the whales and 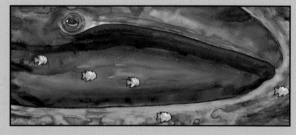 other creatures. By all the nations of the world agreeing not to hunt Gray Whales they have been rescued. You may have noticed the Gray Whale in this book is, in fact, blue. That is because the artist that painted this book just thought he looked better that way. Gray Whales are dark grey/black with patches of white barnacles that make them appear gray.

To learn more, visit Zonk at www.zonktheturtle.com